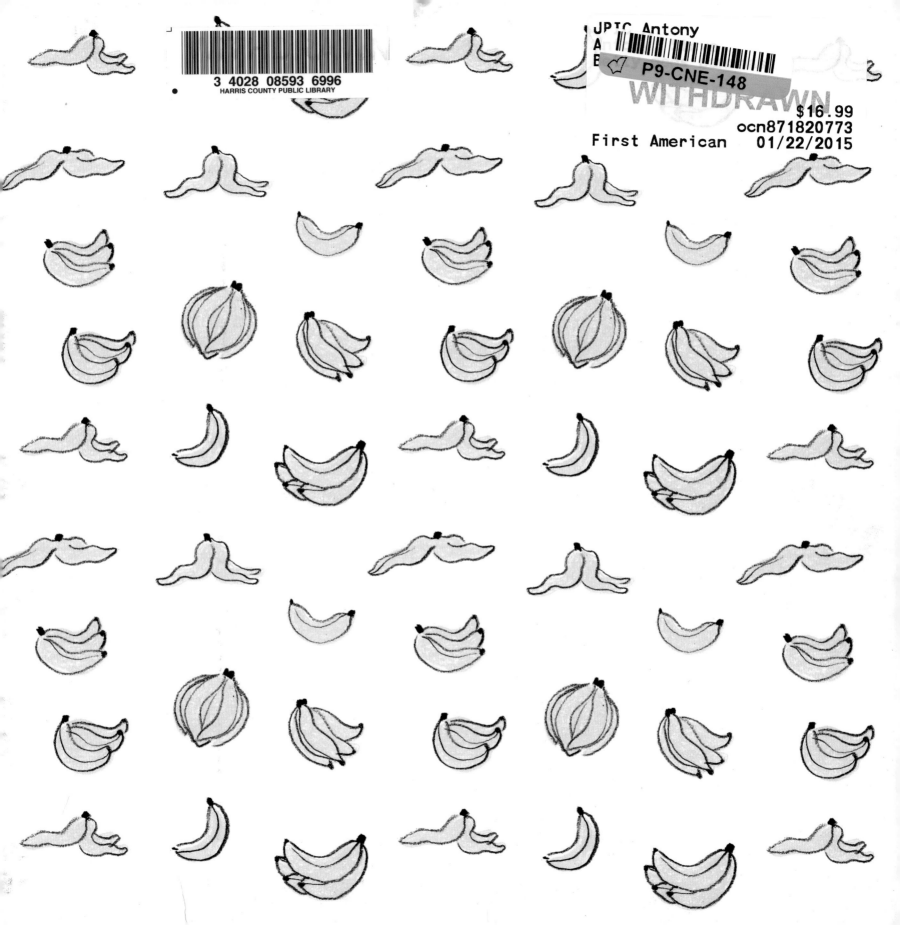

For my niece, Jess

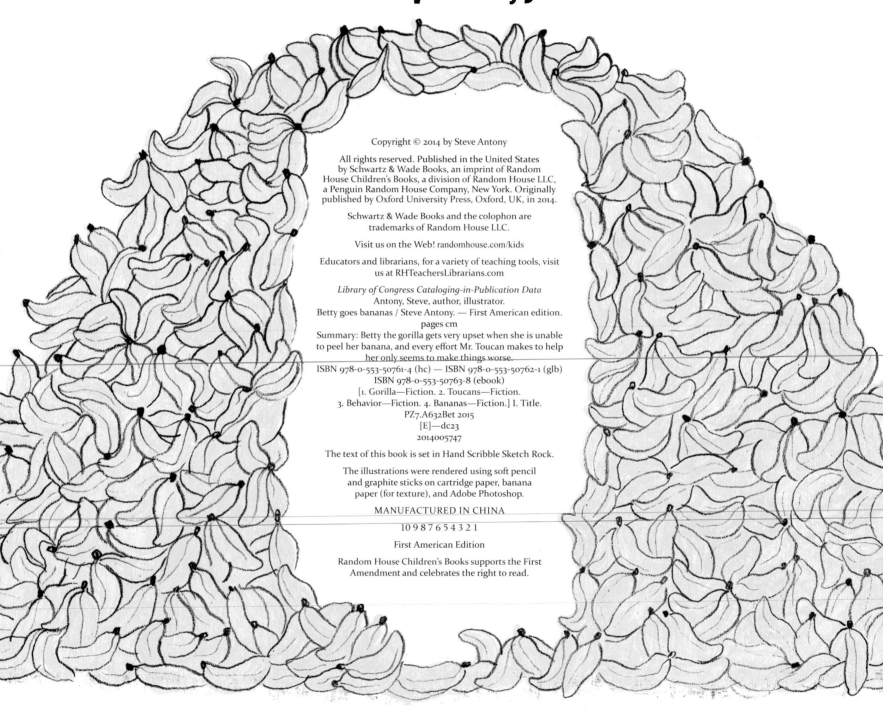

Copyright © 2014 by Steve Antony

Visit us on the Web! randomhouse.com/kids

Educators and librarians, for a variety of teaching tools, visit
us at RHTeachersLibrarians.com

Library of Congress Cataloging-in-Publication Data
Antony, Steve, author, illustrator.
Betty goes bananas / Steve Antony. — First American edition.
pages cm
Summary: Betty the gorilla gets very upset when she is unable
to peel her banana, and every effort Mr. Toucan makes to help
her only seems to make things worse.
ISBN 978-0-553-50761-4 (hc) — ISBN 978-0-553-50762-1 (glb)
ISBN 978-0-553-50763-8 (ebook)
[1. Gorilla—Fiction. 2. Toucans—Fiction.
3. Behavior—Fiction. 4. Bananas—Fiction.] I. Title.
PZ7.A632Bet 2015
[E]—dc23
2014005747

The text of this book is set in Hand Scribble Sketch Rock.

The illustrations were rendered using soft pencil
and graphite sticks on cartridge paper, banana
paper (for texture), and Adobe Photoshop.

MANUFACTURED IN CHINA

10 9 8 7 6 5 4 3 2 1

First American Edition

Betty
goes bananas

Steve Antony

schwartz & wade books · new york

Betty was hungry.
She saw a banana.
She wanted to eat it.

But the banana . . .

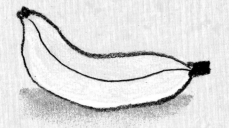

would not open.

Betty tried using her hands,

and her teeth,

and even her feet.

Then suddenly . . .

and
kicked,

and
screamed,

until finally . . .

she calmed down.

"There is no need for that,"
said Mr. Toucan.

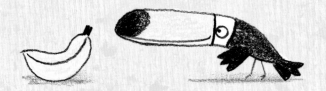

"Watch. I will show you how to peel the banana."

Mr. Toucan showed Betty how to peel the banana.

But the banana . . .

was Betty's, and SHE wanted to peel it.

Betty looked at the banana,   **and looked at Mr. Toucan,**

and looked at the banana again.   **Then suddenly . . .**

Betty cried,

WAAAAAA!

and sniffled,

SNIFF!
SNIFF!

and kicked,

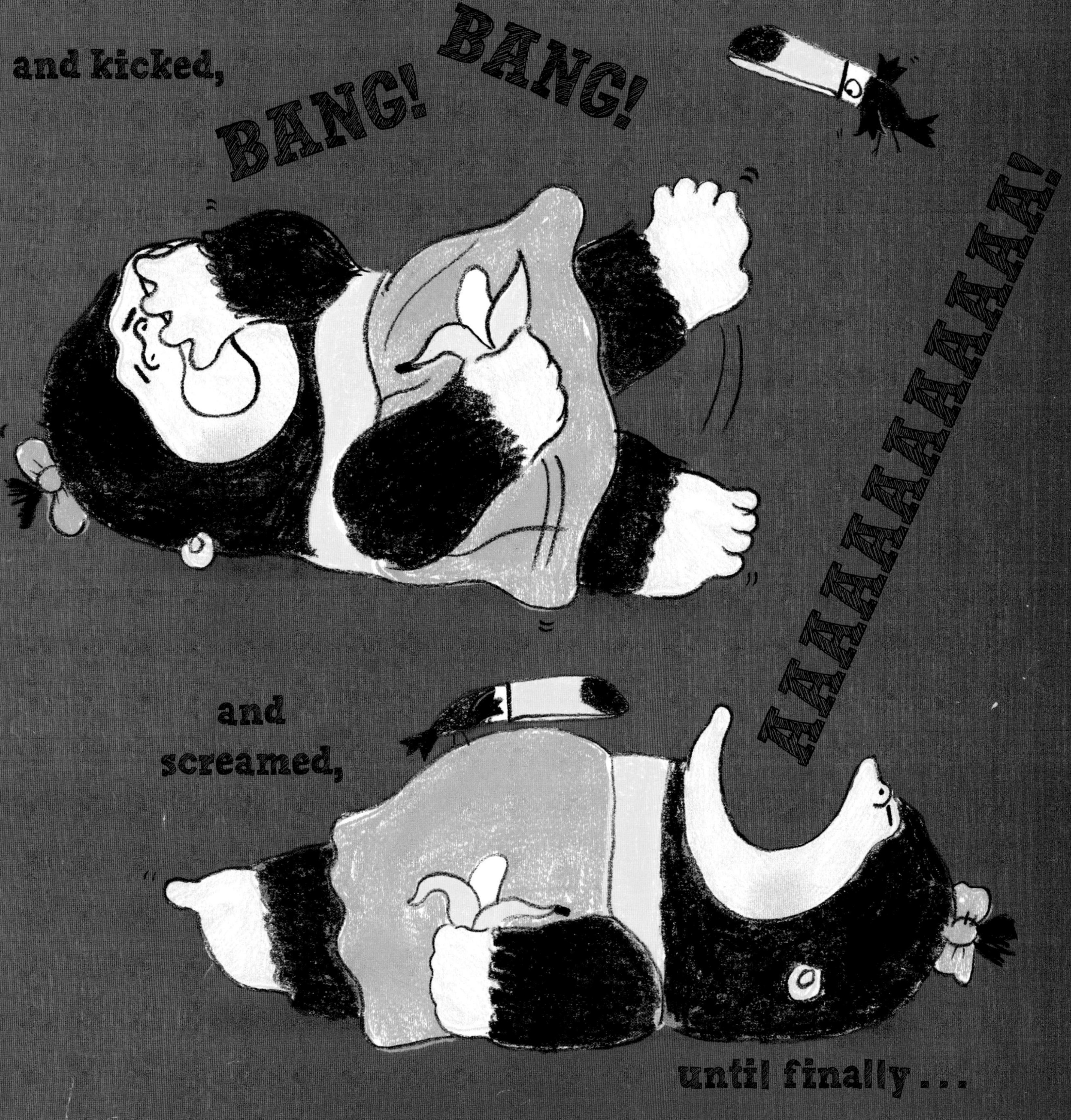

and screamed,

until finally . . .

she calmed down.

"There is no need for that,"
said Mr. Toucan.

"You can peel the banana the next time you have one."

Betty started
to eat
the banana.

But the banana . . .

broke!

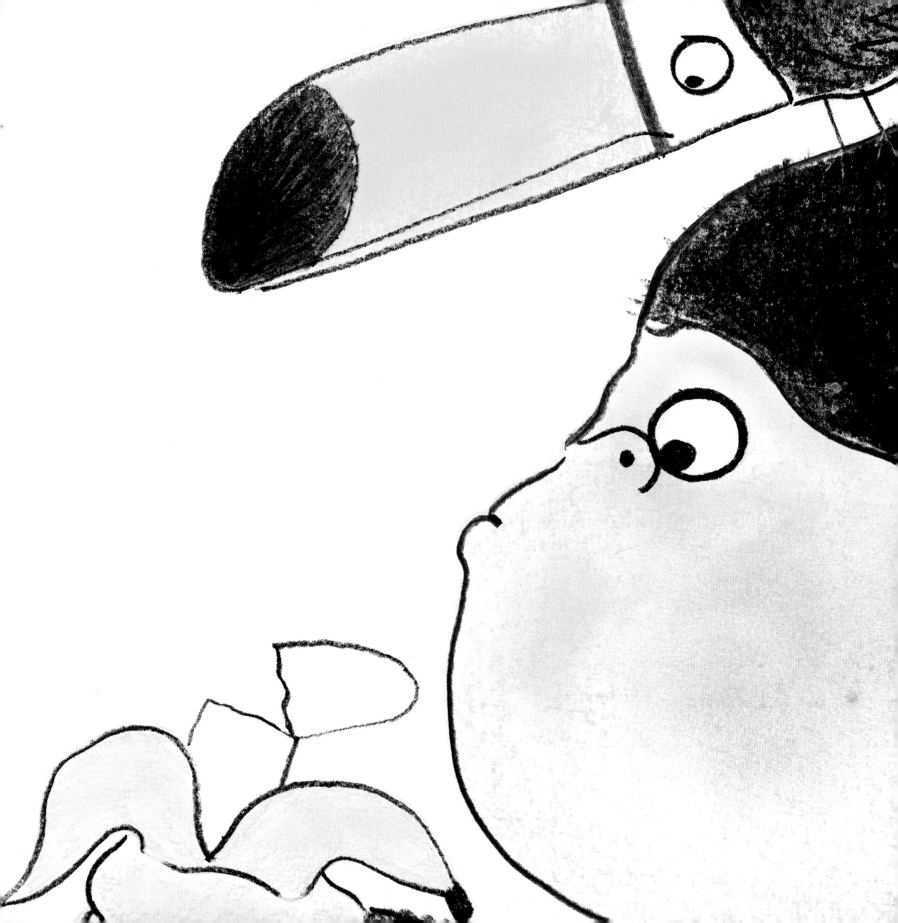

Betty cried,

WAAAAAA!

and sniffled,

SNIFFLE! SNIFF! SNIFF!

and kicked and screamed even louder than before,

BANG! BANG! AAAAA! AAAAA!

until finally . . .

she calmed down.

"There is no need for that," said Mr. Toucan.
"Or would you like ME to have the banana?"

Betty ate the banana . . .

and the banana was

DELICIOUS!

YUM!

Then suddenly . . .

Betty saw another banana . . .